Breakfast of Scallywags

by

Emily Gillespie Clement

http://www.emilygillespieclement.com

Yes! Let's Have Breakfast.

1

Fay LaFarge rolled quietly out of bed and held her breath so she would be skinny enough to squeeze past the bedroom door without making it creak. There was a new, crisp, completely unopened box of Cinnamon Rogers cereal in the kitchen, and she wanted the prize in the package. If she woke up Skipper, who was five, he would pout and whimper and make Mom feel sorry for him. If she woke up Tilly, who was fourteen, Tilly would start her misunderstood teenager drama and make Dad feel sorry for her. But Fay being ten, was neither cute nor misunderstood, and if nobody would look out for her, she'd sure as heck look out for herself.

Like a stealthy, slinky cat, Fay crept down

the stairs, stepping carefully over the third stair from the bottom, which always squeaked. There was just enough morning light that she could see, on the kitchen counter, bright and tantalizing, the fresh box of Cinnamon Rogers.

Sneaking, sneaking, the prize as good as hers, Fay reached for the box.

"Hands off!" shouted Tilly from the hallway. "That box is mine!"

Fay clutched the cereal to her chest, grabbed a wooden spoon, and leapt into position like a swordfighter.

"Not while I'm living!" she cried.

Tilly never sneaked. She stormed. And before Fay could react, Tilly stormed to a strategic position in front of the dish cupboard and turned to glower darkly at Fay.

"You might have the Cinnamon Rogers, but you'll never get a bowl!"

"Scoundrel!" gasped Fay as she faced off on the opposite side of the kitchen table from Tilly.

"I don't want the Rogers," chimed in Skipper, who was thumping down the stairs on his bottom. "They're too cinnanummy. I just want the PRIZE!"

"The prize," said Fay, "is tiddlywinks. You never beat me at tiddlywinks! Are you sure you want it?"

"I want it!" cried Skipper. "And it's called Flippin' Eights, not tiddlywinks!"

"Whatever," said Fay. "but you still want it, even after I saw you trade your apple for a Goober Bar at lunch yesterday?"

"Spy!" said Skipper.

"Sneak!" said Fay.

"No bowl!" growled Tilly.

"Hey!" said Fay, suddenly looking out the kitchen window. "United Delivery is bringing a package...and it's that hot United Delivery guy!"

"No way!" cried Tilly. She ran to the window, combing snags out of her hair with her fingers.

"Thanks for the bowl," said Fay, making a dash for the needed dish, and sliding into a chair at the breakfast table.

Tilly looked disgusted. "There's no delivery guy, you dweeber."

Fay was even more disgusted. "Somebody already opened this box. There's no prize either."

"Wasn't me," said Tilly.

"Me neither," said Skipper.

"Me," said Mrs. LaFarge, walking into the room with baby Lynette on her hip, "I opened it last night. Lynette had an earache. I gave her the tiddlywinks in the box to cheer her up."

"They're not tiddlywinks," said Skipper. "They're called 'Flippin' Eights.'"

"Mom!" scolded Fay. "Lynette's too little for tiddlywinks! She'll choke and die and turn blue!"

"She's almost two," said Mrs. LaFarge, sliding Lynette into her highchair. "Besides, I'll keep an eye on her."

Fay, Tilly, and Skipper looked at each other

in disgust and shared defeat.

"I'm having toast," grumbled Tilly with a scowl.

Mr. LaFarge entered the kitchen, stepping carefully over the bits of cereal Lynette was busily flinging on the floor. He buttoned his white lab coat and adjusted his name badge.

"Don't tell me," he said ."You think Cinnamon Rogers are too cinnamon-tasting?"

"Who cares if she does, Dad?" said Fay, answering quickly so Tilly couldn't. "She can eat plain Jolly Rogers. Don't change the flavor for Tilly."

"Mine Roshers!" squealed Lynette, flinging another handful of cereal.

"They're not too cinnamony, Dad," said Tilly, rolling her eyes. "You're a perfect chief chemist. They're not going to fire you. I just feel like toast."

Mrs. LaFarge picked several stray bits of cereal out of Mr. LaFarge's hair.

"Nobody creates better flavors than you Lyle," she said lovingly. "You have a magic touch. Jolly Rogers cereal is practically addictive."

Mr. LaFarge drummed his fingers on the table. "Toast, toast, toasty sweetness," he said thoughtfully. "Would you say Jolly Rogers have just the right amount of toasty sweetness?"

"Just right," answered Fay. "Except for one thing...Make them put more than one prize in each box."

"That's not my department," replied Mr. LaFarge. "I'm just the flavor guy. But don't expect Mr. Arg to spend money on extra prizes...he's a little tight that way."

"Watch what you say about your boss," warned Mrs. LaFarge, picking more Cinnamon Rogers out of Mr. LaFarge's hair, "because he's...well, your boss."

"Yes, he's my boss," agreed Mr. LaFarge, with a slight shudder. "And what a weird day that was when they put him in charge.

Something about his take-charge attitude is what they said...but he takes more business trips than anyone I've ever heard of..."

There's not much time to dawdle over breakfast on a school morning, so Skipper and Tilly had soon piled their dishes in the sink and gone off to get dressed as Mr. LaFarge left for the cereal factory.

Fay, however, was not concerned with whether her clothes matched, and poured more Cinnamon Rogers into her bowl. Then, something in her bowl went *"clink."*

"Clink," was not the sound she expected from Cinnamon Rogers, so she fished around with her spoon, and scooped out...a quarter. No. It wasn't a quarter. Instead of being round it was not-quite-round around the edges, and there was no eagle, and no *"In God We Trust."* Instead, on one side, was a picture of the sun with its rays pointing to the words *"pass with time or pass time by."*

Fay turned it over. Cool. Very cool. On the flip side a cracked skull lay in two split halves under the words *"either way your time will pass."* Turned out Dad was wrong. Mr. Arg was already putting two prizes in each box, and this time, Fay realized with delight, she had gotten there first. She smiled and, as sneakily as always, put the coin in her pocket.

2

Things were looking ugly at the Crunch & Barley Breakfast Factory as Lyle LaFarge attempted to slip into his flavor design laboratory quietly and unnoticed. Instead, he slipped quietly, and accidentally into the Board of

Directors who were having a heated discussion in the corridor.

"Our stockholders are cranky!" screamed Mrs. Pink, ferociously squeezing a jelly-filled donut which gushed jelly at Lyle LaFarge's name badge.

"We're losing customers to Major Oats and that 'Barnyard Morning Mix,'" moaned Mr. Brown, glumly splashing his coffee on the hapless chemist.

Mr. Green nodded savagely. "Everyone loves 'Barnyard Morning.' Especially the country fig flavor." He gave his fist a furious shake, flinging bits of half-eaten cruller at LaFarge's head.

"No," said Mrs. Pink. "We're not losing customers. In fact, sales are skyrocketing since we hired LaFarge, but we might lose customers if we don't start selling a healthy cereal, like Major Oats!"

"You seem angry," said LaFarge as he tried

to squeeze by, shielding himself with his briefcase.

"Of course we're angry!" shouted Mrs. Pink. "We're the Board of Directors! It's our job to be angry when the company might be on the verge of bankruptcy!"

LaFarge cleared his throat nervously. "According to the profits chart," he said, peeking over Mr. Green's shoulder, "the company is doing very well."

"But what if we're not?" screeched Mr. Green. "What if it doesn't keep up? What if the public only wants healthy food?"

"Like Barnyard Morning," added Mr. Brown.

LaFarge tried to sound reassuring. "All the tasters loved our new Cinnamon Rogers," he said. "We can hardly make enough of it!"

Mrs. Pink scowled. "Kids' stuff!" she said with a huff. "We can't keep Crunch & Barley alive on kids' stuff!"

"What Crunch & Barley needs," snarled Mr. Green, "is something healthy!"

"Something grown-up," added Mrs. Pink.

"Something tasty," mumbled Mr. Brown.

"*LAFAR-R-R-R-R-RGE!*" bellowed a deep and scratchy voice from around the corner.

Lyle LaFarge flinched at the sound of that bellow. His boss's bellow. His boss, the man at the helm of Crunch & Barley, made him nervous, but at the moment anything seemed preferable to another round of donuts. Nodding briskly at the Board of Directors, LaFarge ducked around the corner.

It's hard to say exactly what it was about Mr. Arg that made LaFarge nervous. Certainly it had to do with the way the man's knee-high leather boots pounded the floor as he stomped about the factory. Or maybe the scruffy straw-yellow hair running into scruffier straw-yellow whiskers which had possibly never seen a comb. It wasn't the gold tooth; that didn't bother

LaFarge. But there was something about his boss's right eye, when it fixed on him in an inquisitive glare, that made him feel like a bug on a pin.

"Good morning, sir," said LaFarge, fiddling with the loose handle on the water cooler so he could look down instead of at his Mr. Arg.

Mr. Arg stuck his hand into his coat pocket and jingled some coins.

"Are you ready for this LaFar-r-r-r-ge?" he asked. "Last month it was a plastic spyglass...but guess what we're puttin' in this month? A game in every box of Jolly Rogers and Cinnamon Rogers...a game I made up meself! It won't just be the small fry wantin' that, will it?" Mr. Arg gave a throaty chuckle, then raised an eyebrow at LaFarge who, in order to show good manners, nodded dumbly.

"Sir," began LaFarge nervously, "the Board of Directors feels that we need to introduce something new...something that adults will like."

Mr. Arg's right eye seemed to gleam with raw intensity. LaFarge winced.

"Let's take a walk, LaFarge," said Mr. Arg, doing nothing more than pointing a pen at LaFarge's belly, but as LaFarge walked through a doorway into the cavernous production room he had a sinking sense that he was walking the plank at dagger-point.

Mr. Arg motioned LaFarge onto a metal platform, with steps leading down to the cereal packaging plant. Below them equipment hummed and workers scuttled here and there checking gauges and flipping switches.

"And what," began Mr. Arg in a voice too chillingly polite for LaFarge's comfort, "is wrong, if I may be so nosy, with Jolly Rogers?"

"No offense sir," replied LaFarge warily, "but the Board feels that adults prefer healthful cereals, such as Barnyard Morning."

"Goose food!" spat Mr. Arg. "Horse vittles! And who says Jolly Rogers ain't healthful? It's even got that vittleman...er...vitterman...er, what's that stuff they got in limes?"

"Vitamin C, sir," said LaFarge.

"Rightio!" crowed Mr. Arg. "Viterman Sea! Yer crew won't be gettin' scurvy on Jolly Rogers!"

"Perhaps not, sir," said LaFarge shuddering slightly, "but perhaps you should talk to the Board yourself."

"Pantywaists and floozies!" shouted Mr. Arg. "Got buttercups for brains, everyone of 'em! If it weren't fer that law what says I gotta have 'em, they'd all be swimmin with the sharks! Grown-up cereal...bah! Last year when they handed me this ship Jolly Rogers was good enough...so it's good enough now! Anyways, me men thinks your new Jolly Rogers are better than their granny's Sunday supper."

"Your men Mr. Arg?" asked LaFarge.

Mr. Arg's right eye narrowed, and glared all the more fiercely. "Don't be askin' me about me men LaFarge." He began to mutter to himself.

"Talk to the Board...I'll talk to the Board...pantywaists and buttercups..."

Mr. Arg turned, gave his coins a decisive shake, and promptly split a hole in his coat pocket. A jackpot of coins and other objects clattered across the metal catwalk in all directions.

"Fer the love of Neptune!" cried Mr. Arg. "That's the second time this week me pockets have split!"

LaFarge scrambled to collect the bouncing money and return it to his fuming boss.

"Gots to get me a new jacket...and gots to make me *special tunnel*...the men'll be gettin' restless," muttered Mr. Arg as he shoveled the treasure into another pocket.

"I beg your pardon sir?" said LaFarge, handing over the last handful of coins.

Mr. Arg narrowed his gaze to a withering glare. "Nothin' LaFarge. I didn't say nothin'."

3

Fay headed for school, late as usual, not feeling at all sure what good it might do her to have a cereal box coin in her pocket, but she was certain it must mean good luck. So she was surprised when her teacher, Miss Parsnip, announced that tomorrow's field trip to the Briny Harbor Aquarium (fun) would be postponed, and they would instead visit the Crunch & Barley Breakfast Factory (boring).

But she wasn't at all surprised, while making macaroni mosaics in art class, when Barnaby Hootsman grabbed one of her noodles, stuck it in his nose, then tossed it back into the pile.

So the day hadn't started lucky, but there must be something good about having a cereal box coin that your sister and brother didn't get.

During a group project of making a cell model out of jelly beans, she showed the coin to Jan and Franny.

"Spooky picture," said Jan with a shudder.

"Weird words," added Franny. "Why isn't it round? Who smashed it up?"

"It's not smashed," said Fay, "it's a pirate coin. It came out of the Cinnamon Rogers. It's not supposed to be round."

"Can you spend it?" asked Jan. "I'm saving up for a Dishy Boys cd."

"Can you flip it?" yelled Barnaby Hootsman, snatching the coin out of Franny's hand and tossing it in the air.

What happened next was fast and messy, but it ended with Barnaby on his back, Fay tripping over him, and the coin in Miss Parsnips blazer pocket.

"You know," said Miss Parsnip with a sigh, "Group projects would be so much more productive if we could just focus on our work."

At the end of the day, if Miss Parsnip hadn't been busy showing Judy Fipple how to clean the fish tank, Fay might have been able to ask for her coin back. Instead, by the time she'd listened to Judy Fipple ask Miss Parsnip about eighty-nine show-offy questions, Skipper appeared at the classroom door waiting to be walked home.

So it was in a very grumpy, coinless mood that Fay walked through the front door that afternoon.

At dinner, Mr. LaFarge arranged a handful of tiny vials next to the breadbasket.

"Yuck!" protested Tilly. "I hate when you bring work home with you! You're going to make us taste?"

Mr. LaFarge seemed apologetic. "The Board of Directors wants me to create an adult cereal, like Barnyard Morning."

"Barnyard Morning tastes like a stack of poopy hay," said Fay.

"Pooey hay!" squealed Lynette.

"But adults seem to love its nutty richness," said Mr. LaFarge with a shrug. He held out a dropper from one of his vials. "Try this Cora."

Mrs. LaFarge stuck out her tongue, and Mr. LaFarge gave her a drop.

"Tastes...like a tree," said Mrs. LaFarge with a slight wince. "Tastes like I bit into a tree."

"Oh...no, wrong one," said Mr. LaFarge shuffling his vials around. "That's not the flavor I meant to give you...here Fay, you try this one."

"I don't want to try one," answered Fay. "I always get the ones that taste like doggy doo."

"Fay," said Mrs. LaFarge, "that's not constructive criticism. And if you're that fond of the subject of doodoo, you can just take Lynette upstairs and change her into a clean diaper."

A protest almost popped out of Fay's mouth until she caught her father's stare. He was on the verge of making a speech. Fay hated speeches. She pulled Lynette out of the high chair and headed up the stairs.

"No Pay, go 'way Pay," protested Lynette as Fay laid the toddler down for a change of pants. First, there was the matter of the jar of pureed squash clutched tightly in Lynette's fist. Fay pried it from the toddler's grip and dropped it in her sweater pocket. And luckily, the soiled diaper was merely damp.

There was a bright side to today, thought Fay. At least I missed the taste testing session.

She absentmindedly tucked the rolled up diaper into her other sweater pocket, hoping she hadn't missed dessert.

4

Field trip days were special, and Miss Parsnip always looked ready to lead an army into battle. Today she was dressed in khaki from head to toe, and the pockets in her mesh vest overflowed with tissues, cough drops, and other important provisions.

"Boys and girls," began Miss Parsnip enthusiastically, "As you know Crunch & Barley is one of the largest companies in Elbow Harbor, and many of your parents work there. Who can tell me what product Crunch & Barley is best known for?"

Judy Fipple's hand shot straight up and she cried "ooh ooh ooh!"

"Maybe she ate too much of it," whispered Fay to Jan.

"Jolly Rogers Cereal!" shouted Judy Fipple.

"Make that new and improved Jolly Rogers Cereal," added Fay.

"A pirate-themed cereal," said Miss Parsnip nodding. "Elbow Harbor has always been notorious for its pirate legends. Why it's a well-known story in my own family, that my great-great-great Auntie Bonny Patty Parsnip was a buccaneer who sailed from this very port! So today's field trip groups will all have swashbuckling names! As I call the groups, would you please stand together?"

Anyone who's ever been grouped for field trips knows that there are good groups, and there are bad groups. Fay was hoping earnestly for a good group, though, without her pirate coin she was afraid luck might not be with her.

Miss Parsnip cleared her throat. "In Mr. Hootsman's group, known for today as the Cutthroats, is of course Barnaby. And also, Judy Fipple, Donny Bing, and Fay LaFarge."

Fay's heart did a flip and a nose-dive. There

was nothing good about this. Nothing at all. Disgustingly perfect Judy Fipple, boring Donny Bing,...and the horrific Barnaby Hootsman. The only slight, tiny glimmer of a bright spot was that she would be a Cutthroat. She didn't listen to the rest of the groups as they were called out. She was too busy trying to make sure she stayed on the other side of Donny Bing from Barnaby. Better to be bored to death than to suffer unearthly torment.

"So, Fay," said Mr. Hootsman, his big pumpkin face grinning, "What's your pop do over there at the cereal plant?"

Barnaby grinned too, looking like a miniature version of his dad.

"He makes flavors!" said Barnaby, "Like Booger Banana, and Snotty Seaweed!"

"Hey," said Mr. Hootsman, "you're funny like your old pop, aren't ya?"

Barnaby grinned even more grotesquely.

"Atta'baby," said Mr. Hootsman proudly.

"He's a chemist," stated Fay, thinking about what she might be forced to do to Barnaby if his dad weren't standing there.

"Well," said Judy Fipple. "That's nice, but my mother is a state senator and my father runs the best flower shop in Elbow Harbor, Fipple Floral."

"Do they sell soup?" asked Donny Bing.

Judy wrinkled her nose and looked annoyed. "It's a flower shop," she said, "they sell flowers."

"Oh," said Donny, "well, I really like soup. I try to think of a new soup idea every day."

Fay tried not to grit her teeth out loud. I will get through this field trip, she said to herself. I am a Cutthroat.

5

Mrs. Pink took her job as chairperson of the Crunch & Barley Board of Directors very seriously. If anything fishy was happening at the factory, she would sniff it out. Sniffing was the thing she did best. And today, Mrs. Pink had sniffed out a whopper. Her fishiest fish yet.

"What?" demanded Mr. Green, stomping huffily into the boardroom. "What's important enough to interrupt my donut break?"

"Yeah," muttered Mr. Brown with a slosh of his coffee, "this better be good."

"Good," said Mrs. Pink icily, "is not quite the word we're looking for." She slapped a stack of paper onto the table. "Take a look boys."

"It's the production record," said Mr. Green. "Duh."

"Duh indeed," said Mrs. Pink. "Showing

how many boxes of cereal were produced last month."

Mr. Brown flicked the top paper aside and stared gloomily at the second page. "This is how much we shipped out," he said.

"Correct," stated Mrs. Pink. "And if you subtract the number of boxes shipped, from the number of boxes produced, you should get the number of boxes we have in the warehouse."

"Wait," said Mr. Green punching numbers on a calculator. "That's ten thousand boxes. And at twenty boxes per crate..."

"Five-hundred crates," said Mr. Brown. "We should have five-hundred crates in the warehouse."

Mrs. Pink squinted and nodded her head. "Come with me," she said.

Mr. Green and Mr. Brown hustled to keep up with Mrs. Pink's clicking heels as she led the way to the warehouse. She stopped in front of a metal door, turned the handle, and threw it open dramatically.

"Have a look," she said.

The room was cavernous and so empty it echoed. There was just one small stack of boxes in the corner.

Mr. Brown began to count on his fingers. "Ten crates," he muttered. "Only ten lousy crates."

"Preposterous!" exclaimed Mr. Green. "Not to mention improbable! What happened to the other four-hundred and ninety crates?"

"Gentlemen," said Mrs. Pink. "I suspect that the only person who can answer that question is Mr. Arg."

"Did he eat them?" asked Mr. Brown.

"Did he secretly sell them and pocket the cash?" asked Mr. Green.

"All we know," responded Mrs. Pink, "is that if he did sell the cereal, some of the profit rightfully belongs to our stockholders, who chose us to keep Mr. Arg on the up and up. And if Mr.

Arg can't give us a good explanation...then gentlemen, we're looking at theft. We're looking at cheating. We're looking at corporate fraud. What we're looking at, in a word gentlemen, is...*piracy!*"

6

After an orderly march from Elbow Harbor Elementary, down Elbow Street, with a sharp right turn on Cargo Point Road, Miss Parsnip came to a halt in front of the Main entrance to the Crunch & Barley Breakfast Factory and blew several blasts on her sailor's whistle.

"Ahoy!" she said. "Are all my groups on deck? Cutthroats, Rogues, Peglegs, Swabbies? All here? That's shipshape! Let's go in and see if our tourguide is ready for us!"

But there, framed in the doorway as Miss Parsnip pulled it open, was Mrs. Pink, clicking a high heel on the floor in a rapid staccato beat.

"I'm sorry to say, there won't be tours today," said Mrs. Pink, her tone clipped and snooty.

Miss Parsnip looked understandably perplexed. "That can't be the case," she said. "We're officially signed up. All the proper phone calls were made."

"Be that as it may," replied Mrs. Pink, as if that settled the matter once and for all.

"Oh," said Miss Parsnip, seeming uncertain about what she should do next. "Oh. I see."

Intending to get the attention of her students and their chaperones, Miss Parsnip blew her whistle. Miss Parsnip was an excellent teacher who rarely forgot anything, but at this moment she did. She forgot that two toots meant "attention," and three toots meant "forward mateys." Miss Parsnip blew three toots. And before she could add four toots, (meaning "change of plans,") the twenty fifth-graders of Elbow Harbor Elementary poured through the doorway like water gushing from a broken dam.

"Mr. Green!" called Mrs. Pink irately as she tried not to get swept away in the tide of ten year olds. "Mr. Brown! This is a very poor day for a tour group, do you not agree?"

"Thar's NO SUCH THING as a poor day for tourin' on a vessel o'mine!" came a booming voice from the top of a short flight of stairs.

Mr. Arg strode toward the now very disorganized mob of students, and doffed his feathered hat.

"That," whispered Fay to Franny, "is my Dad's boss. Mr. Arg."

"And are the wee folk whisperin' because they want a mop," drawled Mr. Arg fixing his right eye on Fay, "or are ya' so excited that the willies are eatin' holes in the part of yer head that knows manners?"

"Sorry sir," said Fay.

Franny merely quivered.

"But Mr. Arg," cut in Mrs. Pink, pushing Judy Fipple aside to confront him. "Our meeting. Our important meeting!"

"CAN'T YA' SEE," began Mr. Arg in a roar that dwindled to a growl, "that I'm showing me factory to a group of little children? Alrighty then, who's in charge here?"

"I am," said Miss Parsnip stepping forward as Mrs. Pink stood gaping. "I'm the teacher, Arlene Parsnip."

"You're in charge?" said Mr. Arg.

"Yes," said Miss Parsnip.

"No ma'am," said Mr. Arg with a swagger and tip of his hat. "This here's my factory...and

I'M in charge."

Fay had never seen Miss Parsnip blush so red before, and she tried not to giggle.

"MR. ARG!" said Mrs. Pink. "I'll will be reporting this!"

"Report any bloody thing ya' want, scurvy wench," snarled Mr. Arg before turning to the school group. "And now a tour," he said, "the likes o'which you swabbies have never seen before."

7

Fay glanced around the shiny industrial hallways of Crunch & Barley and felt a meager glimmer of hope. Visiting the cereal factory had to be the most tedious field trip she could think of, especially in Barnaby Hootsman's group, but with the notorious Mr. Arg leading the tour...maybe, just maybe it would be better than she thought.

"This here," said Mr. Arg opening a door that led to the noisy cereal making equipment, "Nah...this part's boring...it's just our mixin' room where we...uh...mix spices an' all that...and over there's where...uh...well where the spices meet up with the doughy part...and, uh, grub's over thar' across the hall."

"Grub?" asked Miss Parsnip politely.

"Vittles," responded Mr. Arg. "Sustenance." He lowered his gaze as if sharing a company secret with Miss Parsnip. "Ya' gotta let yer' crew eat, Missy, or they git mutinous on ya'."

Most surprisingly, Miss Parsnip blushed again.

"At school we call that lunchtime," she said, mirroring Mr. Arg's secretive tone.

"So wee ones," said Mr. Arg, "do ye' have any questions?"

Donny Bing raised his hand. "Do people here ever have peanut butter soup for lunch?"

"Soup?" sputtered Mr. Arg looking bewildered.

"Fresh flowers would make the lunchroom more cheerful," volunteered Judy Fipple without waiting to be called on.

"Sure, if yer' a buttercup," snarled Mr. Arg who turned to continue the tour.

Five extremely boring minutes and eight extremely boring rooms later, Fay was forced to admit that Barnaby Hootsman was making some sense for a change.

"Hey Mister," called out Barnaby, "when do we see something good, like, I don't know...the garbage dumpster?"

Several students tittered, and Mr. Hootsman clapped Barnaby on the back and said "atta'baby."

Mr. Arg's dark gaze focused narrowly on Barnaby, but he continued his tour, ignoring the interruption.

"Wait," continued Barnaby, sniffing loudly, "Smell that? We must already be near the dumpster!"

Mr. Arg stopped. A machine behind them merrily dropped prizes into boxes passing on a conveyor belt. But an outbreak of chuckles from the students faded into dead silence as Mr. Arg turned around. His gaze bore into Barnaby Hootsman like a drill.

"Yer too young for a pistol," began Mr. Arg

in a lilting growl, "so I can't maroon ya'...but I can give you a chore befittin' one with your mouth...so boy, START SWABBIN'!"

Barnaby's face whitened and he stammered, "w-w-with what?"

"With a MOP ya' varmint!" bellowed Mr. Arg. "Go on! Git! Go find a mop!"

Barnaby glanced at Mr. Hootsman, who shrugged then nodded. With a return shrug, Barnaby scrambled up the metal stairs and through the doorway which slammed behind him with a ringing clang.

"Wait a bloomin' minute...," said Mr. Arg giving his yellow beard a tug. "I almost forgot me own buddy rule...gots ta' send a buddy with the rapscallion."

Fay had just noticed, with some disgust, that she still had a dirty diaper and a jar of pureed squash in her sweater pockets when Mr. Arg bellowed, "You!" It wasn't until he added, "the little missy who likes ta' whisper too much," that

she realized he was pointing at her.

"Yes you," said Mr. Arg when Fay looked up. "Catch up with the scoundrel and see that he finds a good swabbin' mop!"

Fay just nodded her head. And feeling not at all certain where Barnaby had disappeared to, she turned around and ran up the metal stairway and through the clanging door.

8

Barnaby was right about one thing--Crunch & Barley was a smelly place. But not a bad kind of smelly. It was more like being inside a big box of Cinnamon Rogers. Not bad at all. Fay paused in the shiny tiled corridor to listen for any Barnaby-like footsteps, but only heard swooshing liquids and clinking glassware from a room up ahead. She peeked into the room, but there was no Barnaby--only a lanky man in a white lab coat pouring orange liquid from a flask into a bubbling beaker

"Dad," said Fay. "Nice lab you got here."

"Hello," said Mr. LaFarge. "Fay, did you lose your class?" A jar on a burner behind him began to spit and smoke.

"No," said Fay, "I didn't lose them. I'm looking for Barnaby Hootsman. Mr. Arg sent him to get a mop."

Mr. LaFarge hastily pushed the spitting jar off its flame, glanced at his watch, said "yikes," and gave the orange bubbling beaker a hasty stir. A pan on a hotplate began to hiss yellow steam. Mr. LaFarge quickly turned down the heat.

"Dad," said Fay, "Where's the person who helps you?"

"Good question," replied Mr. LaFarge, "Mr. Arg has him working on some kind of 'special project,' which must be very important, based on how loud Arg hollered."

"The more important, the louder?" asked Fay.

"So it seems," said Mr. LaFarge. "Hey, there's a janitors' closet at the end of the hall. Maybe your friend found it."

"Thanks Dad, I'll check," said Fay ducking out of her father's flavor lab.

The janitors' closet was locked. And Barnaby was nowhere to be seen, unless he was locked inside, which wouldn't be a bad thing at all. Or maybe he was stuck in the freight elevator at the other end of the hall, which was making loud *bing bong* noises as it stopped first at the basement, then at the roof, then at the basement again, in annoying repetition.

Fay was certain that an elevator would never behave this way if the person riding in it had actual work to do. She suspected foul play, and foul play almost always meant Barnaby Hootsman was involved. Fay ran to the elevator and punched the call button. A few bings and bongs later the doors opened, and she was looking at Barnaby's grinning face.

"Want a ride?" hooted Barnaby. "Only five bucks!"

"Where's your mop, Hootsman?" asked Fay, leaning against the elevator door to keep it from closing.

"Mop department," called Barnaby, "second floor, to the left!" He pushed the button marked two. Fay felt the door closing against her back and she jumped inside the elevator so Barnaby couldn't get away again.

At floor two, the elevator lurched to a halt, and the door sprang open.

"There better be mops here," snarled Fay.

"You already lost me my pirate coin...you're not getting me into any more trouble."

"Oh the coin, the precious coin," began Barnaby in a singsong lilt. *"Fay LaFarge has lost her coin!"*

"Mops Hootsman!" demanded Fay. "Where are the mops?"

"This-a-way!" squealed Barnaby, taking off down the hall at a run. He slid to a halt in front of a metal door. "Right in there," he said with a dramatic flourish.

"Hootsman," said Fay, "you're going to die young." She pushed open the door for Barnaby, then followed him through.

The noise was almost deafening. In front of them, a conveyor belt clicked by, carrying large stainless steel pots of a gooey oat mixture which Fay guessed was cereal dough. Pistons thumped noisily up and down to keep the belt moving.

"No mops Hootsman," shouted Fay looking around. "But at least there's a garbage can so I can lose the stinky baby food." She pulled Lynette's squash out of her pocket and tossed it in a lazy arc at the trash can. A lazy arc which was intercepted by Barnaby Hootsman.

"Yum yum!" said Barnaby with a grin. "You throw like a girl! Can't let nutrition go to waste!" He popped the lid off the squash and emptied the contents into one of the moving stainless steel pots.

Fay merely rolled her eyes in disgust before pulling Barnaby back out into the hallway by his shirt collar.

"It's swabbing time Hootsman," she said scanning the hallway. A wooden door across the hall was narrower than most of the others, and Fay felt certain it must be a closet.

But it was not a mop Fay saw when she flung the door open with her free hand. It was a chubby man in blue coveralls, furiously stuffing handfuls of trash into the door of an old-fashioned cast-iron furnace.

9

"Got more mass?" grunted the man looking up from the furnace. The room was swelteringly hot, and in one glance Fay could see why. The iron furnace, roughly the size and shape of a dishwasher, was so hot that the strange and unrecognizable markings that decorated it almost glowed.

"What?" asked Fay. "We're looking for a mop. I thought this was a broom closet."

"I didn't think it was a closet," said Barnaby. "This place stinks. I don't think they ever clean around here."

The man's face was glistening, and the collar of his coveralls was wet with perspiration. He had evidently been working hard for some time, and he looked utterly discouraged.

"It is a broom closet," said the man. "Well, a utility room anyway." He slammed the cast iron door and turned toward Fay and Barnaby. The name-patch on his coveralls said "McCorley-- Flavor Lab."

"Flavor lab..." said Fay, "Do you work with my father, Lyle LaFarge?"

"Ha," said McCorley ruefully, kicking at the corner of the hot furnace. "I did. Then I opened my big mouth."

"Join the club man, I do that all the time," said Barnaby with a grin. "Did you get into trouble too?"

"I'm an idiot," replied McCorley. "It was nonsense. When I heard Arg say something about a "special tunnel", I thought about wormholes and this stupid comic book I read about warping time. So I made a stupid crack that if he wanted a really special tunnel all he needed to do was condense enough mass. So he sticks me in this room and says, 'There ya' go

McCorley, let's see how much stuff ye' can cram in there!'

So now I know he's cracked."

"Mr. Arg?" said Fay.

"Yeah, Mr. Arg," answered McCorley. "He's a fruit loop if he really thinks I can make a wormhole."

"What's a wormhole?" whispered Barnaby.

Fay shrugged.

"It's fiction," said McCorley. "It's bad science fiction. Condense enough matter and you get a black hole. Preposterous--but at least I get paid vacations."

"Hey," said Barnaby. "We'll help you! Shoveling crud is our specialty!"

Fay gave Barnaby a withering glare.

"Seriously," said Barnaby, "It's gotta be better than more of that lame tour!"

For the second time that morning, Fay found herself in the awkward position of agreeing with Barnaby.

"Okay fine," she said, "let's shovel...um...what kind of stuff are we looking for?"

"Baby food flavored cereal," snickered Barnaby.

"Or you could jump in there Hootsman," said Fay.

"Naw," said McCorley. "Garbage. Dust. Anything you find. Just bring it all back here. The more the better. We've just got to make it look like I'm trying."

"Alriiiiight!" said Barnaby taking off into the hallway. He ducked through an open doorway into a mail sorting room, followed closely by Fay.

"Garbage collection time!" shouted Barnaby grabbing the nearest wastebasket.

"Wait," called a lady was feeding envelopes into a stamping machine, "Don't forget the shreds!" She tossed a fat garbage bag of shredded paper at Fay.

McCorley shrugged when Fay and Barnaby

returned to the broom closet. "Okay," he said with a chuckle and an eyeroll. "Not much density there, but here goes."

McCorley opened the cast iron door with an oven mitt. The glow from inside was so hot the air wobbled, and he shook the bag of shredded paper in the general direction of the opening. Fay fully expected most of it to scatter and hit the floor. But it didn't.

There seemed to be something sucking the paper into the furnace, almost like a vacuum, and as it swirled through the opening McCorley tapped his foot and chanted, *"Ooooh yeah...go baby go...ooooh yeah...go baby go...ooooooh...,"*

He trailed off and shook his head. "Isn't this fun kids?" said McCorley. "Nothing like getting paid to be a trash incinerator! Looks like we need more mass!"

"Mr. McCorley?" asked Fay. "Isn't that thing going to fill up with ashes sooner or later?"

McCorley looked back blankly. "Well I

guess," he said. "But as far as I can tell it's all still in there."

Barnably shrugged. "More mass!" he hollered, charging back into the hallway.

"More mass," repeated Fay, right behind him.

By this time Fay had gotten into the spirit of things. She grabbed a mailcart from nextdoor, and by the time she got back to the broom closet with Barnaby at her heels, they had collected two bags of shredded paper, a bucket of cigarette butts, and three sacks of yesterday's smelly lunchroom trash.

McCorley shoveled and chanted as Fay upended the cigarette butts near the furnace door, and they had a real dump and shovel rhythm going as Barnaby followed with the shredded paper. The lunchroom trash stunk like a dumpster as Fay and Barnaby each grabbed a bag and dumped.

Fay's head felt light, and the room wobbly

as the last tray of unfinished coleslaw disappeared into the opening.

"Eww...my Dad's feet!" she heard Barnaby yell. Fay just coughed and wobbled with the room as she heard McCorley's chant change to *"oh geez...I think I got a vortex...oh geez...I think I got a vortex...oh geez..."*

Fay's head cleared. The room was quiet.

"No vortex," said McCorley dejectedly. "But I got a headache. And a stack of bills I can't pay when Arg fires me."

Stomping feet clattered in the hallway. Feet stomping in heavy knee-high boots, followed by a lighter step, trotting to keep up.

"Ye' shoulda' told me yer' varmints were troublemakers!" shouted Mr. Arg from outside the door. "Running around me fact'ry like they own the place, the scurvy critters!"

"Mr. Arg!" retorted the voice of Miss Parsnip indignantly. "My students are very responsible! And dependable! It was you who sent them off to get lost!"

The door flew open. Mr. Arg's glowering face fixed first on Fay then on McCorley.

"Harborin' stowaways are we McCorley? And how 'bout me little tunnel...or wormy hole ...or whatever then?" demanded Mr. Arg.

"With all due respect sir," answered McCorley, "there's not enough trash in Elbow Harbor..."

"Children," cut in Miss Parsnip, "it's time to rejoin the class."

"Not enough trash McCorley?" shouted Mr. Arg, his face turning red. "And I say yer' an incompetent boob!"

"And I say," muttered Fay, suddenly remembering the squishy used diaper in her sweater pocket, "yuck. Here's some more mass Mr. McCorley!"

She gave the diaper a quick heave toward the open furnace door, grabbed Barnaby by the shirt collar, and turned to follow Miss Parsnip.

But she couldn't move. Her feet refused to do as she wished. Nor could she move her arms. In fact, she had no choice at all but to be sucked backward toward the toward the center of the broom closet as Mr. Arg and Miss Parsnip stretched and spiraled toward her like wisps of smoke.

10

After a moment of fog-headed dizziness, Fay landed with a bump on her bottom in the middle of the room.

"Ow!" cried Barnaby Hootsman from behind her. "My Dad's suing your pants off if I got all burned up!"

"This...isn't the broom closet," said Fay, looking around.

The Crunch & Barley green linoleum was gone; now the floor was wooden planks. It seemed more like a shed than a closet, and a dusty shed at that.

McCorley lay propped on his elbows, staring dazedly at the ceiling. Miss Parsnip was on foot, hands on hips, and the look on her face meant the class was in for a good talking to.

Only the class wasn't here. Fay guessed that Mr. Arg, who was straightening his coat, would get the talking to instead.

"Well McCorley," said Mr. Arg calmly. "Ya' done it. I knew ya' could."

"Geesh," replied McCorley. "Geezowhizzo...what the heck happened?."

"The same thing as always happens with

that accursed forge! That's why they call it accursed!"

"Mr. Arg!" cut in Miss Parsnip sharply. "It is completely unacceptable that the dangerous rooms in your factory aren't plainly marked! It is not good for children to be subjected to such jolts!"

"Malarkey," replied Mr. Arg, as he rummaged distractedly through his pockets. "Ya' can't break a kid."

"This field trip is over," stated Miss Parsnip. "Fay, Barnaby, we will return to the class at once. We're going back to school."

"Not bloody likely," said Mr. Arg, "As you can plainly see, the forge didn't come with us, but be my guest." He gestured toward the door.

Miss Parsnip glared first at the door, then at Mr. Arg.

"That's not the door we came in," she stated.

"That thar's the only door," said Mr. Arg with a chuckle.

Fay shrugged, turned the handle, and looked out. The Crunch & Barley corridor was gone...in fact, the whole factory was gone. There was nothing but wind and sunlight pouring in from a shipyard. A smelly shipyard full of horse droppings and unbathed men. Fay was used to smelly babies who needed baths, but she wasn't prepared for the huge man with a pock-marked face who was grinning at her with pointy yellow teeth.

"I hope yor' not the only fing the cap'n brung back wif 'im," said the smelly man with a pointy-toothed leer.

Fay slammed the door.

"Take us back," she said. "Now."

"Ya' can't go back Missy," said Mr. Arg with a smirk. "That was a one-way trip. Do you see any other ways out?"

Fay looked toward the center of the room. Empty. No trash. No furnace.

"My Dad's suing your pants off if I'm stuck

here," said Barnaby.

"Well sonny...yer' Dad's not suing me or nobody fer' now," replied Mr. Arg, "'cause he ain't been born yet, and neither has your grandpappy! I'll see you folks later...I'm off to rejoin me crew."

Mr. Arg jingled the coins in his pocket, gave a wistful sigh as if something was missing, and left the shed. Miss Parsnip stomped after him indignantly as Fay peeked around the doorframe at the shipyard, then took a step outside.

"You will at least," demanded Miss Parsnip, "point us in the direction of Elbow Harbor!"

Mr. Arg smiled at Miss Parsnip as if she were a silly little girl, and pointed inland. A crooked green store, with a crooked front porch stood at the end of a very short road. On the store was a sign with the letter "P" and a picture of a white carrot. A few ramshackle houses were clustered around the store, and at the other end of the very short road, where Fay, Barnaby, Miss Parsnip, McCorley and Mr. Arg now stood, was the smelly shipyard, with its old boats, oily ropes, and a few odd sheds.

"Welcome to Elbow Harbor," said Mr. Arg.

11

"What nonsense," said Miss Parsnip as Mr. Arg stomped away. "I hope that rude man knows that I'll be reporting this to the school board and the Chamber of Commerce."

"Report the smell too," said Barnaby. "Peeeyoooo."

"It's just horses Hootsman," said Fay.

"Plus pirates with no deodorant," snorted Barnaby.

"Oh, they're not real pirates," said Miss Parsnip. Her usual enthusiasm seemed to be returning. "They're called re-enactors. They dress up to teach people what pirate life was like."

"To smell what pirate life was like," added Barnaby.

"Yes," agreed Miss Parsnip. "Very authentic. In fact, if you two wait right here I'll go ask them if they could appear at our school for Pirate Day."

"She is so totally obsessed with pirates," said Fay as Miss Parsnip trotted off briskly.

"What's the matter Fay? Don't you believe in 'Bonny Patty Parsnip,' the lady pirate?" asked Barnaby in a tone that Fay didn't find at all respectful.

"I believe in Barnaby Hootsman the deck swabby," said Fay.

"You a swabby?" grunted a demanding

voice. Fay turned to see a scrawny man in a bloodied apron clutching a meat cleaver and staring at them.

"I need a swabby," he said, "to clean up the feathers an' gizzards an' such."

"Well," said Barnaby, looking a little nervous, "I need a Coke...to quench my thirst and such."

"And I bet," said Fay, "they sell them right there at that store. You coming Hootsman?"

Something hit the back of Fay's leg with a *"plink."* She turned. A red-haired pirate was concentrating very hard at popping a small coin into a tin cup by pressing on it with a large coin.

"Flippin' eights," said Barnaby. "They're playing flippin' eights!"

"Scram ya' little Missy Pattycake!" yelled the grizzled old pirate next to the red-head. "Ya' messed wif' me shot!"

"Sorry," said Fay. She took off toward the green store. When Barnaby caught up he looked at her with fake concern.

"But, Fay LaFarge, our teacher Miss Parsnip told us to wait for her back there, with the stinky men."

"Right Hootsman," replied Fay, "As if she won't be able to find us. Anyway, did you want chicken-man to start butchering you?"

Ahead of them, the door of the white carrot store swung open with a creak and a woman's voice bellowed from inside.

"Off with you scalawag law-breakin' rum-swillin' pirates!" bellowed the voice, "unless you're sure your head's tougher than my skillet!"

"Take it easy lady," said a bald man with a lizard tattoo who was backing onto the porch. A shorter man followed him on tiptoe.

"I never take it easy with vermin," snarled the young woman in the long gingham dress who was holding a cast iron pan as if it were a baseball bat.

"That'a girl Patricia," cackled an older man

behind the woman with the skillet. "Show 'em ya' mean business!"

As the pirates scuttled off the porch, Patricia's attention turned to Fay and Barnaby, and she lowered her pan. "Do you young folks need something?"

Fay had a feeling the woman might be nicer if she hadn't just been shooing away scalawags, but the pan still made her a little nervous.

"Coke?" suggested Fay.

The old man hooted and coughed. "This ain't coal-minin' country little miss," he cackled. "What'd your mumsy send you for? New clothes? Or is girls dressin' up like hurdy-gurdy farm-boys the latest from Paree?"

"Okay," said Barnaby, "how about soda?"

"That's inside," answered Patricia. She held the door open. "Come on in."

"What the heck kind of store is this?" asked Barnaby in a hissing whisper as they entered. Fay shushed him instead of answering. Because she didn't know. The room was full of wooden bins and jars, and nowhere did she see what she really craved--a cooler stocked with cold drinks.

"Don't mind all the ruckus," said Patricia as she hung the skillet from a hook on the wall with some other assorted pots. "Those pirates have been getting out of hand this last week or so. Those two just came barging in here like bulls in a glass shop tellin' me they want cereal. I show'em rolled oats and they got all unruly, like they think I must be hiding something better."

"They oughta' be puttin' out to sea soon," said the old man, nodding.

"They'd better," said Patricia. She opened a flap on the top of a barrel and held up a scoop of white powder. "Soda's right here," she said. "Doing the wash today?"

"No," said Barnaby, "soda..you know, like...the kind you drink?"

Fay suddenly remembered her mother tossing baking soda in the washing machine to get odors out of Lynette's barfy baby clothes..

"Oh, I get it," she said knowingly. "You're showing us what things were like in...what year is this supposed to be?"

Patricia looked at her oddly. "This is seventeen-hundred and eleven. Supposed to be and it is."

"Not to be rude or anything," said Fay, "but is there a real store nearby?"

"Yeah," added Barnaby, "with refrigerators...not like the White Carrot here."

"Carrot?" replied the old man, with another cackle. "Don't you know your vegetables, boy? That's not a carrot, that's a parsnip. Like our name. I'm Joe Parsnip and this is my little girl Patty."

12

"Your name is Patty Parsnip?" Fay asked, looking at Barnaby to see if he was thinking what she was thinking.

"Bonny Patty Parsnip?" asked Barnaby.

"Well, if you say so," replied Patty with a grin, "but that's a little fresh for a boy your age."

"And you really think this is 1711?" asked Fay.

Patty nodded. "Last I checked it was," she said.

"And you really don't have a Pepsi?" asked Barnaby.

"A whatsy?" asked Joe Parsnip. "Did you two just get off a boat from Shangree-la or somethin'?"

"Can't be that," cut in Patty. "Haven't been

any new boats in this port since Captain Arg and his scurvy crew took up residence."

"Captain Arg?" asked Fay. "Mr. Arg is the captain of those pirates?"

"Yup," said Joe Parsnip. "Ol' Yellerwhiskers."

Fay noticed Barnaby sizing up Patty with his usual stupid, trouble-making grin.

"Bonny Patty Parsnip...aren't you supposed to be a pirate too?" he asked.

"What boy?" replied Patricia indignantly. "First you're fresh, now I don't know what you're getting at!"

"Please," said Fay. "Ignore Barnaby. You're obviously not a pirate."

The front door of the store squealed open and Mr. McCorley, the flavor-lab man stumbled into the room.

"Pirates!" squawked McCorley looking around wildly. "And I think they're real!"

"Of course they're real," said Patty. "I

should know. They've been disrespecting my store since they made berth in Elbow Harbor."

Again the door squealed, and this time the scrawny cook with the bloody apron shuffled in.

Patty put her hands on her hips. "Mr. Twicky!," she said. "Have I not made myself perfectly clear? You have cleaned us out of basil and bay leaves! There are no more herbs until the boat comes from Boston!"

"Ain't ya got any tarragon?" asked Mr. Twicky.

Patty was quickly losing her patience. "No tarragon!," she said, vigorously stacking jars of assorted vegetables on a shelf. "No oregano. No rosemary. No parsley. We don't even have any cinnamon!"

Mr. Twicky began to twitch. "The boys is tired o'plain chicken," he said. "They's tired of chicken soup, chicken fricassee, chicken pie, and fried chicken. They's tired of chicken!"

"Um, duh?" said Barnaby. "Fix something

that's not chicken."

"Ain't got nothin' left boy!," complained Mr. Twicky. "Exceptin' me Pappy's special hardtack...and they don't even want it!"

"What do they want?" asked Fay.

The answer came like the first rumble of thunder before a storm. "We want Rogers!" yelled the unison voice of the mob of pirates which seemed to be coming from just outside the Parsnips' store.

Soon the rumble became a steady chant. *"Jolly Rogers, Jolly Rogers, Jolly Rogers!"*

"They sound pretty antsy," said Fay. "Do you think they're dangerous?"

Patty didn't look as calm as she was trying to sound.   "Usually that Captain Arg of theirs keeps things under control, but he's been gone a while and they're getting restless."

"Mr...um, Captain Arg is back," said Fay reassuringly. "He came with us."

But the chanting was getting frighteningly

loud.

"Jolly Rogers, Jolly Rogers, JOLLY ROGERS!"

"Maybe we oughta' hide in the root cellar," suggested Joe Parsnip.

Barnaby piped up. "I'm assuming you don't sell Jolly Rogers here?" he asked hopefully.

"Don't know what it is, sonny boy," replied Joe Parsnip.

"It's that crunchy stuff what the Cap'n's been bringin' 'em," offered Mr. Twicky. "And now they won't eat chicken. Or me Pappy's hardtack."

"Barnaby, " whispered Fay. "Did Arg have any cereal with him when we got here?"

"Uh, I don't think so," replied Barnaby.

"JOLLY ROGERS, JOLLY ROGERS, JOLLY ROGERS..."

The chanting was louder, more insistent, and now it seemed to be right on the front porch. And this time the front door didn't open with a squeal. It exploded inward, popping right off its hinges, as an angry mob of pirates screaming *"JOLLY ROGERS"* gushed through the opening.

13

Fay stumbled over a flour sack and Barnaby almost fell into the pickle barrel as the room filled with sweaty, snarling sailors. The big yellow-toothed pirate whom Fay had first seen at the shed door was now sneering into her face.

"What'cha got ta' eat here Missy?" he demanded. "Gots ta' be better'n Twicky's hardtack!"

"You have tried my patience long enough sir!" said Patty stepping forward to square off with Yellow Tooth. "You have eaten everything we have, and I say it's time for you and your nasty shipmates to set sail!"

"Plus you stink!" shouted Barnaby Hootsman from over by the pickle barrel.

Fay wished he hadn't. Because a glimmer of craziness suddenly appeared in Yellow Tooth's eyes which hadn't been quite so obvious before.

"And just how pretty are you gonna smell," snarled Yellow Tooth, "in pickle juice?" Snagging Barnaby by the shirt collar, Yellow Tooth hoisted him in the air, then dunked him head first into the pickle barrel. Barnaby scrambled to right himself and came up sputtering as the pirate crew began to chant *"FOOD FOOD FOOD FOOD!"*

"OUT!" yelled Patty.

"You first!" hollered Yellow Tooth pushing her into the pirate mob, which kept pushing her right out the door.

"You too Codger!" yelled Yellow Tooth, as Joe Parsnip was shoved out right behind Patty.

But just as Yellow Tooth fixed his crazed glare on Fay, she heard a familiar growl from the doorway.

"What ARE ya?" bellowed Captain Arg. "Squirmy little Mommy's boys? Weentsy little babies havin' a tantrum 'cause their Mama won't give 'em sweetsies?"

A hush fell over the room as Arg shoved his way to the center of the crowd.

"You ain't gonna tell me," said Captain Arg, "that you big boys are startin' a riot on account of you run out of Jolly Rogers, now are ya'?"

The other pirates' growls softened to a simmer. Yellow Tooth alone seemed to have no intention of backing down.

"I wanna know Cap'n!" he demanded. "About the Jolly Rogers. Are we out? Or are we flat out?"

Captain Arg returned Yellow Tooth's fearsome stare without a blink.

"I'd like to know what difference it's going to make," he said, "whether we're out, or whether we're flat out?"

"The difference," said Yellow Tooth, unsheathing his cutlass with a swish of metal, "has to do wif' whether I filet you now...or later!"

Arg looked surprised, but only for a flash, as he drew a sword of his own.

"You ain't shiverin' my timbers, boy," he said. "I'll feed the crew what I want, when I want."

A murmur started from the pirate mob, and a lone voice from the back squeaked "so long as it's Jolly Rogers!"

"Jolly Rogers!" cried another voice, followed by another, until the entire mob was droning in spine-tingling tones, *"JOLLY ROGERS JOLLY ROGERS JOLLY ROGERS..."*

"And who hasn't got no Jolly Rogers boys?"

snarled Yellow Tooth with an evil curl of his lip.

"*ARG!*" screamed the crew.

"Skewer 'im!" yelled a pirate.

"Roast 'im like a bull on a spit!" shouted another.

Fay winced and shut her eyes tight as glass broke behind her. She opened them again to see a surging mob of pirates gone mad--smashing windows, spilling cabinets, and one heaving a lit tobacco pipe at a bolt of canvas which caught fire like an exploding gas can.

The door was nearby. If she ran now she'd make it out. *But what about Barnaby?* She'd barely had the thought when something that felt like a bird's claw gripped her arm and pulled her out the door.

14

Two overwhelming and disagreeable smells assaulted Fay's nose when the claw released her on the sand outside the store. The pickle smell was Barnaby whose arm had been clutched in Mr. Twicky's other claw-like hand. And the bloody apron, which she now found herself uncomfortably close to, reeked of rancid chicken fat.

"The boys is gettin' a little rowdy," said Twicky.

"Rowdy?" sputtered Barnaby. "They're completely psycho! They're wackers!"

"I think," panted Fay, "that 'Captain' Arg has lost control of his crew."

Behind them, at the Parsnips' store, a

window smashed from the inside, and smoke billowed from the side door. Pirates, whooping and snarling, formed a ring around the building.

"Children," called the frantic voice of Miss Parsnip. "It's time to go! I'm sorry to say this exhibition has become a bit too realistic for safety sake!"

"Where are we going to go?" asked Fay.

"Anywhere but here!" shouted Mr. Arg as he dashed from the store and made a beeline for the shed they'd started out in.

"Follow that man!" cried Miss Parsnip.

"You ain't kiddin'," added Twicky.

Fay took off, with Barnaby, Miss Parsnip, and Mr. Twicky right behind.

As they lunged into the shed, Fay slammed the door, and Mr. Twicky threw the bolt into place.

"So now what?" asked Fay. "They burn the shed down too?"

"We'll be french fries!" screamed Barnaby.

"Don't care if they do, and don't care if they don't," growled Mr. Arg, "so long as I find my piece o'eight." He began frantically patting his jacket. "Gots to be here somewhere...stuck in the lining or something..."

"Your pizza what?" demanded Barnaby.

"Piece o'eight boy! That accursed piece what was forged in the accursed furnace what got us here today! If I got the piece o'eight I don't need that cast-iron hell hole!"

Outside the shed, Fay heard a gruff and mocking voice.

"You in there, Cap'n? You're missing the paaaarrrrty..."

"Piece o'eight...piece o'eight...," muttered Mr. Arg.

WHAM! Something heavy collided with the door, rattling the whole rickety shed.

"Give yourself up!" squawked Barnaby. "Maybe they'll bargain!"

The voices outside the shed grew louder.

Evidently, the mob had abandoned the burning store and was regrouping here.

"The Captain's not here!" yelled Fay, hoping to buy time. "He's on the ship!"

"Piece o'eight...piece o'eight..." Mr. Arg continued to mutter. He turned his jacket inside out and began to shake it.

"YAAARGGG!," yelled a voice outside the door, "Mess wif' me an' I'll eat your eyeballs raw! We know the Cap'n's in there!"

BOOM! Something hit the door harder.

"Cap'n?" squeaked Mr. Twicky. "Ya' think it's the best time to be worryin' about money?"

"I NEED MY PIECE O'EIGHT!" roared Mr. Arg who was now ripping the lining out of his jacket.

"A piece of eight is money?" asked Fay, as a thought crept into her head. "As in...a coin?"

"Oh sure, oh yeah," said Barnaby sarcastically, "I bet those psychos would be happy to leave us alone for...a COIN!"

Mr. Arg stopped shredding his coat and glared at Barnaby.

"It ain't just any piece o'eight ya' guppy," he said. "It's an accursed thing...but it's the only thing!"

BASH! The door started to creak.

"Miss Parsnip!" called Fay, trying hard not to panic. "Do you still have my pirate coin?"

"Your what, dear?" asked Miss Parsnip.

"My pirate coin," repeated Fay. "The one you took away when I was fighting with Barnaby."

CRASH! The door splintered and began to give way.

"Oh," said Miss Parsnip with a nod of recognition. "Yes, that. You know, dear, you could really use some anger management coaching."

More wood cracked with a horrific squeal, and Fay saw Yellow Tooth, leering hideously at her through a dinner plate sized hole in the door.

"Honey, I'm home," he said. "Hope you set

the table real pretty."

Miss Parsnip shook her head as if she disapproved of the face in the doorway and removed a coin from her purse. "Is this what you're looking for dear?" she asked. "Do you think you could be more careful with it from now on?"

Fay was certain there was no time for respectful behavior. She snatched the coin from Miss Parsnip's outstretched hand, and handed it to Mr. Arg. "Will this help?" she asked.

"Blow me over with a tin whistle!" cried Mr. Arg. "Me piece o'eight! How'd you...oh never mind that..."

Yellow Tooth's hideous face had disappeared from the hole, replaced by the butt end of a log, smashing into the door with full force. As the hole grew larger, Mr. Arg crouched and fingered a knothole in the wooden floor.

"You lubbers'll stand near me if you know what's good fer ya'," he said distractedly.

The log hit what was left of the door with a

mighty whack. The door was gone. Mr. Arg dropped the coin into the knothole, and Fay knew that, once again, she was being sucked toward a tiny point in space--only this time, the face stretching and swirling behind her was pockmarked and had yellow teeth.

15

The coin hit the floor with a *"plink."* Fay hit the floor with a *"bump."* This time it was the green linoleum floor of the Crunch & Barley broom closet. Fay felt relief...for a few seconds. Then she felt smothered as the tiny room filled to the corners with putrid pirates, jostling each other for every square inch of wiggle room.

"Arg set us a trap!" growled one squashed and outraged pirate.

"We fell in a hole!" snarled another.

"Get off my foot Fatso!" yelled Barnaby.

"Blast and bloody cod-livers," muttered Mr. Arg. "me piece o'eight...whar'd it go now..."

Fay made herself small and squeezed between one pair of legs, then another until she reached the door. But before she had time to open it, it abruptly opened itself. She flattened herself against the door frame as Mr. Green, of the Crunch and Barley Board of Directors, was knocked rudely off his feet by Mr. Arg bolting out of the closet.

"Why don't you ask him if you can have your coin back now?" snickered Barnaby, squeezing into the hallway beside Fay.

"Because I'm not a psycho with a death wish," Fay replied.

"That's ok," said Barnaby with a smirk, "I'll ask him for you! Mr. Arg?"

"ARRRG!" growled Yellow Tooth jumping into the hallway, and unsheathing his cutlass.

"MISTER Arg!" barked Board of Directors chairperson Mrs. Pink, stepping sharply into Mr. Arg's path to block his escape. "WE are due for a SERIOUS discussion about the quantity of Jolly Rogers presently in the warehouse!"

"Jolly Rogers?" cried Yellow Tooth. "In the warehouse? Where be this warehouse?"

Mrs. Pink looked coldly at Yellow Tooth and sniffed. "Employees only. And please put away that sharp object."

"Where be the Jolly Rogers?" demanded another pirate as the remaining eleven staggered into the hallway.

"WHERE?" bellowed Yellow Tooth as the ghastly crew formed a ring around Mr. Arg and Mrs. Pink.

Mrs. Pink showed no fear. "Employees ONLY," she repeated insistently.

"Rrrrrrrrrg..." The twelve pirates began a

rumbling growl, and drew out daggers and cutlasses.

Mr. Brown, peeking around a bend in the corridor, was visibly quivering. "First floor, end of the hall, green metal door!" he said. "Please don't kill me! I'm only thirty-four!"

Yellow Tooth stood tall and grinned a nasty yellow grin. "Have at it mateys!" he shouted. The pirates stormed toward the stairwell in a clanking stampede.

Mrs. Pink glared at Mr. Brown with a look that would wither a tree, then turned to confront Mr. Arg. "Now you've done it," she said. "If you think four-hundred and ninety missing crates were trouble, how do you intend to replace five-hundred?"

"Lady, that's not half the problem," said Fay. "What happens when the cereal is all gone?"

"All gone," twittered Mr. Twicky, hobbling out of the broom closet. "That's when them varmints'll have to settle fer' Pappy's hardtack.

Or chicken. Ooh! I like this place! Squeaky clean!"

Mr. Arg fingered his beard and shook his head. "With ol' Yeller Tooth in command of them scallywags there's no tellin' what'll happen. All's I can say is...Elbow Harbor better brace itself."

Elbow Harbor better brace itself? Fay wondered how dangerous Yellow Tooth and his foul crew could be.

The hallway's harsh fluorescent light glinted gold off the floor by the broom closet doorway. Fay quietly reached toward the source of the flash and, once again, stashed the pirate coin in her pocket.

16

"Miss Parsnip!"

It was Judy Fipple calling from the end of the corridor. "Miss Parsnip!" repeated Judy. "We were completely unable to find you. For almost two hours!"

"Barna-baby!" cried Mr. Hootsman, holding out his pudgy arms for Barnaby.

"Miss Parsnip," said Donny Bing. "I brought potato wedge soup. Would now be a good time to eat it?"

Miss Parsnip looked rumpled and attempted to straighten her hair.

"Why don't you eat it at school?" she replied distractedly. "We're going back to school. Right now. Are all my groups present? Cutthroats? Rogues? Peglegs? Swamis....slobbies, um...oh...just everyone? Let's move!"

Fay fell quietly in line behind the relieved parents and students and considered Mr. Arg's warning. There were some rough characters on the loose, no question about that. But how much trouble could they possibly get into in modern day Elbow Harbor?

Well, Fay thought, *at least I was wrong about the field trip to the Crunch & Barley Breakfast Factory. It wasn't quite as dull as dust after all.* And now she had the pirate coin bouncing in her pants pocket again. But it was time to go back to school. Back to boring Elbow Harbor Elementary.

Miss Parsnip led the way out of the factory toward Elbow Street. Normally boring Elbow Street, but now buzzing and hopping with activity. People were running in out out of buildings, and all three dedicated officers of the Elbow Harbor police force were hastily jotting notes in their police officer notebooks.

"They took daisies," whined Horace Fipple who was standing by the front door of Fipple's Floral in a green apron. "And floral arrangement supplies! You can't just take supplies! All our arrangements are custom made by professionals!"

"That's outrageous!" exclaimed Judy Fipple, raising her hand in the air. "Miss Parsnip, may we stop and assist the police in this investigation?"

"Children!" replied Miss Parsnip with alarm in her voice. "We are not criminologists! We would surely be in the way! We will get back to school at once!"

"But Miss Parsnip!" called Barnaby Hootsman. "We can identify the culprits!"

"What's that?" piped up the police lady who'd been questioning Horace Fipple. She stared at Barnaby Hootsman. "You have information about these hoodlums?"

"Maybe," replied Barnaby. "Is there a reward?"

"Atta'baby," said Mr. Hootsman thumping Barnaby on the back. "Sock it to'em."

"May I have your name," asked the lady cop, pointing her pencil at Barnaby.

"Hootsman," replied Barnaby in his best secret agent voice. "Barnaby Hootsman."

"And has anyone else witnessed suspicious characters in town, besides you?" continued the cop.

"Would I have to split the reward?" asked Barnaby.

"Hootsman was with me," said Fay stepping around Judy Fipple. "We both saw 'em."

"And you would be?" asked the police lady.

"Fay LaFarge," said Fay.

"Ma'am," said the police lady to Miss Parsnip. "We'd like to borrow these two students for now, so they can help us make sketches of the perpetrators."

Behind her, a timid little police artist with a clipboard nodded and waved his pencil.

"Fay," asked Miss Parsnip, "Barnaby? Are you all caught up on multiplying fractions?"

"One-third times one-fifth equals one-fifteenth," replied Fay.

"That goes double for me," added Barnaby.

"Fine then," said Miss Parsnip. "Hurry back to school so you can copy down tonight's assignment."

"Okay kids," said the police lady, "I'm Officer Brambly. Would you say this gang has a leader?"

"That would be Yellow Tooth," said Fay. "The meanest, ugliest scoundrel you'd ever care to lay two eyes on."

"In your worst nightmare," added Barnaby.

"And his teeth," continued Fay, "are yellow. And pointed like a row of daggers."

The timid little man nodded and sketched vigorously.

"Nasty skin," continued Fay, "looks like popped bubble wrap."

"And body odor," said Barnaby, "that'll make you drop dead."

The little man stopped sketching. "I don't think can draw that," he whispered.

"Sure you can," replied Fay grabbing his pencil. "Just make some squiggly lines coming from him to show stink...like this."

"And put a dead guy next to him," added Barnaby grabbing the pencil from Fay, "with x's for eyes...like this..."

"Oh," said the little man, obviously pleased. "Oh yes, that does the trick."

Fay and Barnaby described the other twelve pirates in gruesome detail from their stubbly whiskers to their wrinkly tattoos, until it was clear the police artist was happy with his results.

"I don't want to go back to school for fractions," said Fay. "But if I don't take my lunchbox home tonight my locker will smell like old putrid tunafish."

"Oooh," said Barnaby with an evil gleam in his eye. "Old putrid tunafish! What if it accidentally gets loose in Judy Fipple's desk?"

"What if it doesn't?" replied Fay tartly.

"What if I get to school before you?" challenged Barnaby, before taking off at a run.

"What if it gets loose in your hair Hootsman?" shouted Fay. Fay tore down Elbow Street after Barnaby, overtaking him at the edge of the schoolyard, where they both skidded to a halt.

Fay stared at the playground. "Hootsman," she whispered. "I think we're too late."

17

Fay dodged behind the kindergarten shuttlebus and pulled Barnaby after her.

"That is not Mr. Clobbins, the PE teacher," said Barnaby, with a snort.

"And those kids are not playing kickball," said Fay.

They crouched behind the front wheel, peering over the nose of the bus.

Fifteen first-graders, who were normally taught very good manners by their teacher, Mrs. Gulbert, were now being taught very bad manners by a fat bald pirate.

"TAKE THAT YA' SLITHERING SLIME-EATER!" yelled fifteen first-graders in unison.

"Good!" yelled the fat pirate. "GOOD! Now

swing your cutlass, like this!"

Fifteen first-graders gave their daisies a mighty swing and petals flew everywhere.

"That's al'right," said the fat bald pirate encouragingly, "but it'll look better when we fix you up wif' real blades."

This is not good, thought Fay. Not good at all. Sure, Mr. Clobbins' fitness drills were deadly boring, but first graders with swords were likely to chop their babysitters' feet off.

"I'm going to try to get inside," whispered Fay, edging toward the front of the bus.

"Do you have a screw loose?" squeaked Barnaby. "They've probably barbecued everyone else by now! You'll never come out alive!"

"Still," said Fay. "What if I can do something? You can go get the cops or come in. Your choice, I don't care."

Fay looked back at the bald pirate with the first-graders. They were standing in a circle holding what was left of their daisies in the air and making ferocious faces at each other. She hoped their growling was loud enough to drown out her footsteps as she made a dash for the cafeteria workers' door.

Squeezing through the door, careful not to squeak...she was inside! Then she froze. There were at least three pirates right here in the kitchen. She flattened herself against the giant steel refrigerator where the lunch ladies kept ice cream.

A gangly pirate with a curly red ponytail was looking out

the window with a Jolly Rogers cereal box plastic spyglass. "Cain't see no-one," he said. "Must've been Jimbo out thar' with the wee ones."

"Well then he oughter' shut up a little," growled an old pirate with bad teeth, who was squinting as he tried to squidge a little plastic coin into his flippin' eights cup with a big plastic coin.

"What...you wanna' give me them flippin'

eights and you go teach them babies Hanky?" chuckled a bearded, brown-skinned pirate.

Hanky snarled and headed for the refrigerator. Fay slid for the dishwashing sink and ducked under it.

"I'm gonna eat them babies, if'n I can't find anything better 'round here," replied Hanky, giving the refrigerator door an aggressive yank.

He gave a disgusted grunt. "Still nothin' in this, whatchacallit, Friggy-dairy but that slimy cold stuff that makes me teeth ache," he grumbled. "We gots to find us some more Jolly Rogers."

Hanky slammed the refrigerator door and trudged over to the window. Fay scrambled on all fours from the sink to behind a stack of lunch trays. Then from the lunch trays to underneath a table. From a table to another table. From the table to the hallway.

A short, bony pirate with a Jolly Rogers spyglass was keeping guard at the school entrance across from the cafeteria. Every so often he took some practice swings at the cardboard policeman who always stood just inside the main door.

Feeling confidant about her sneaking skills, Fay slid quietly along with her back to the lockers until she was surprised by an open locker door which slammed with a bang.

For a moment she froze, alarmed that she'd be spotted. But it was not pirates who began to clammer and yell. It was the teachers, all of them, and the school principal, Mr. Squibbly, who were locked in the supply closet and wanted out now.

She peeked through the small window in the door and shrugged at them. I can't let you out yet, she told them by mental telepathy, even though she was quite certain they didn't understand. You'd end up skewered.

Teachers in a closet is not such a bad thing, Fay assured herself. But keeping kids at school unnecessarily late is completely unacceptable.

Fay could think of only one thing to do. But she'd have to get into the school office without being seen by the bony pirate. There had to be a way to distract him. Very quietly she opened the locker door behind her and felt around. Perfect. An orange. A nice squishy moldy orange.

Fay got a good softball grip on the orange and rolled a speedy grounder at the cardboard policeman. As Mr. Officer fell flat on his face, and the skinny pirate gaped at him in surprise, Fay made a silent sprint for the school office and ducked behind Mr. Squibbly's desk.

Reaching up, she felt for the loudspeaker microphone from the desktop, pulled it down and made herself comfortable on the floor.

"Get ready to have your timbers totally shivered, you boneheads," whispered Fay.

18

Luckily, Fay had been the morning announcement reader last Thursday. She knew exactly which button to push on the microphone to make sure she would be heard by the entire school.

She took a deep breath and pushed the yellow button. *"AHOY YOU GOOGLE-EYED SCUMSUCKERS!"* Fay hollered into the microphone in her deepest voice. She sneaked a peek at the bony pirate in the hall. He looked startled, like a deer in headlights. Fay smiled.

"THIS IS THE GHOST OF DAVY JONES!" she continued. *"YOU KNOW WHO I AM! I'M THAT DUDE THEY NAMED THE LOCKER*

AFTER!"

There were frantic footsteps in the hallway, and loud exclamations as the pirates tried to make sense of the mystery voice.

"YOU CROSS-EYED BOOGERHEADS!" Fay bellowed into the microphone. *"DIDN'T YOU HEAR THAT BELL? IT'S MORALLY IMMORAL TO MAKE CHILDREN STAY AT SCHOOL AFTER THAT BELL RINGS! YOU BETTER LET'EM OUT NOW, OR I'LL HAUNT YOU AND HAUNT YOU UNTIL YOUR BOAT SINKS FASTER THAN THE TITANIC!"*

More muttering in the hallway.

"What's th'Titanic?" said a gnarly pirate voice.

"Ta' heck if I know," replied the unmistakable, but slightly nervous, voice of Yellow Tooth, "but it don't sound pretty. Hanky, Buttercup...let these guppies outa' here. They'd have made lousy recruits anyways."

There was running and cheering in the

hallway, as all one-hundred and fourteen students of Elbow Harbor Elementary, minus Fay and Barnaby, streamed from their classrooms and out of the building. Judy Fipple carefully stood Mr. Officer up on her way out.

Fay heaved a big sigh, and peeked over the edge of Mr. Squibbly's desk, while she waited for the right moment to sneak out and blend with the rest of the kids. Her feeling of relief was, unfortunately, short-lived.

"My dad's gonna sue your pants off!" came a whiny voice from the hallway outside Mr. Squibbly's office.

"Blimey Yeller!" exclaimed Buttercup, the bony pirate. "If'n it ain't one o'them brats what knows Cap'n Arg!"

"And yer' gonna help us find the Cap'n," said Scratchy, the red-haired pirate. "Aren't ya'? So's we can make a new anchor outa' him."

Fay peeked over the desk. Yellow Tooth had Barnaby in the air by the shirt collar, as several members of his grimy crew pointed and chuckled.

"And you know what?" cried Barnaby. "You're not gonna like having your pants sued off! And you know what else? You stink! And you're stupid! You really thought that wasn't a ghost, didn't you?"

"Thought what was a ghost?" growled Yellow Tooth.

"That voice," cackled Barnaby, still suspended by his shirt collar. "You dummy! That was Fay LaFarge talking on Mr. Squibbly's microphone! You're not as dumb as a post, you're dumber!"

"No Hootsman," hissed Fay, desperately fearing her cover had been blown. "You're dumber."

Maybe the pirates didn't even know who Mr. Squibbly was. Maybe they still wouldn't find her. Maybe...there wasn't the blade of a cutlass pointing right at her nose. But there was.

"Well well," said Yellow Tooth in a slow,

ugly drawl. "Looks like we found Davy Jones. And he ain't even in his locker!"

19

Fay backed away from the repetitive jabbing motions Yellow Tooth was making with his cutlass until she found herself next to Barnaby in the hallway.

"So boys," said Yellow Tooth with a horrible, leering grin. "Looks like we've got our recruits after all!" He chuckled and lowered the cutlass, but continued to stare mockingly at Fay and Barnaby. "I hope you pups like looting and ransacking."

Jimbo, the fat bald pirate, sniffed and wiped away a tear. "I've never had children of me own," he said.

"They ain't children any more!" crowed Yellow Tooth. "They're pirates!" He brandished his cutlass at Fay and Barnaby once more. "And they're about to prove it!"

Fay did not like the sound of that at all. Would she have to get a tattoo? Or worse, a pegleg?

"How do we prove we're pirates?" asked Fay. Maybe a show of cooperation would buy her a chance to escape.

"Well, first off, " said Scratchy. "We're gettin' powerful hungry! You gots to help us stock up. On provisions."

"That's right," agreed Jimbo with a fatherly smile. "Feed yer' crewmates, be brothers forever."

"I'm not sure you were brotherly with Mr. Twicky," observed Fay.

Yellow Tooth swung around, his sword cutting the air with a whoosh. "Twicky's a numbskull!" he bellowed. "He can't fix nothin' but chicken and hardtack! What we need is Jolly

Rogers!"

"Cinnamon!" yelled Scratchy.

"Plain!" chimed in Jimbo.

"It don't matter what kind!" concluded Yellow Tooth. "So long as it's got that crunchy goodness!"

Barnaby had been silently glowering at the pirates, but now his mouth curled into a smirk.

"So why don't you crunch on back to the cereal factory?," he said. "Or did you pig it all up when you were there before?"

"I told ya' we shouldn't of been so piggy-hoggy," whined Scratchy to Jimbo with a sniff.

"Maybe the guppy don't understand the life of a pirate," said Yellow Tooth with a glint in his eye. "Maybe he don't know just how hungry we get what with all the raiding and looting."

Scratchy and Jimbo nodded their heads vigorously.

"Maybe," continued Yellow Tooth, "We need to show 'im."

Scratchy and Jimbo nodded harder.

Yellow Tooth stretched to his full towering height and pointed his cutlass at Barnaby. "So get moving boy!" he roared. "Lead the way to more Jolly Rogers!"

"I'm so proud," said Jimbo wiping another tear with a dirty fist. "Their first assignment."

For a moment, Barnaby just stood gaping dumbly at the fluorescent school lights glinting off the blade of Yellow Tooth's cutlass. It seemed to Fay that the usual crazed gleam in the pirate's eyes was growing gleamier and crazier, until *WHACK!* The cutlass, in a motion too swift to catch, had cleanly sliced Mr. Officer's cardboard head from his cardboard body.

"Go now boy," Yellow Tooth suggested.

Barnaby went. With Fay and the pirates right behind.

20

"Hootsman," Fay hissed, catching up with Barnaby as he rounded the playground swingset and took off down Hogan Street. "Where the heck are you going?"

Barnaby panted but didn't slow down.

"Get cereal!" he huffed. "Where else?...Guy's a freak!...he's gonna whack my head off!"

"NO CHATTERIN' IN THE RANKS!" bellowed Yellow Tooth. "And slow down a wee! Me men need to save a little energy for the lootin' part of this raid!"

Barnaby did slow down. Then he stopped. Right on the front lawn of a house with green shutters, where a plastic deer gazed mutely at its reflection in a green gazing ball.

"This is your house Hootsman," stated Fay.

"Duh," said Barnaby. "And we eat Jolly Rogers at my house."

"This be a storehouse for Jolly Rogers?" demanded Yellow Tooth, as several other pirates took swings at the plastic deer.

"It be," said Barnaby, still panting. "In the cabinet next to the refrigerator," he said.

"The what?" asked Yellow Tooth.

"The fridge!" replied Barnaby.

"The WHAT?" demanded Yellow Tooth.

"The friggy-dairy!" snapped Fay. "The big cold thing!"

"Well then," said Yellow Tooth in a calmer, but no less menacing voice. "Lead the charge boy!"

Barnaby shrugged, then yelled "CHARGE!" Fay was right behind him as he barreled into the kitchen where Mr. Hootsman was eating a cold-cut hoagy and staring at the news on tv

"...the band of criminals," said the tv, *"now on the loose in the vicinity of Elbow Harbor is considered armed and dangerous..."*

"Need some food Dad!" called out Barnaby as he rifled through the cabinets.

"Attababy," said Mr. Hootsman, without looking up. "Always work up a good appetite at school. You show'em!"

"...citizens are advised to stay in their homes and lock the doors..." droned the tv.

Jimbo, Scratchy, and the other pirates were clogging up the kitchen doorway until Yellow Tooth pushed his way through and snatched the three boxes of Jolly Rogers Barnaby had pulled from the cabinet.

"Three?" demanded Yellow Tooth. "Three blasted gorsh-forsaken boxes?"

Mr. Hootsman looked up from the tv and squinted at the huge, ugly man blocking his kitchen doorway. Then he looked back at the tv screen, which was currently displaying police sketches.

"Barna-baby," he said. "You've joined the outlaws?"

Fay glanced at Yellow Tooth, who's lip was starting to curl into a sneer.

"They're hungry Pop," said Barnaby with a shrug.

"A dang sight hungrier than three dinksy little boxes," growled Yellow Tooth ominously. "I think we need more." He turned his glare on Fay. "Now it's your turn Missy Loud-mouth. Here's hopin' you can do better."

For a moment, Fay looked at Yellow Tooth's cutlass and considered her options. She could refuse. But the likely result would be a headless Mr. Hootsman, and that would not improve him much. She could run away, but one direction was blocked by a hungry band of scallywags, and the other by Mr. Hootsman who, again, would likely end up headless if she used him for cover. The thought was too gruesome to contemplate.

"Oooookay," said Fay with as much enthusiasm as she could muster. "Let's go troops!"

21

Fay had two strong but competing instincts. The first was to lead Yellow Tooth and his mangy band as far from her house and family as she possibly could, like a bird drawing a predator away from its nest. On the other hand, if she were a spider she'd trap them in her web. Where else but in her own house did she know the territory so well?

Fay felt more like a spider than a bird, so at the crossroads of Hogan and Clover Streets, she took a speedy right, heading straight for the yellow bungalow at the end of the block.

She paused before stepping onto the front

porch and turned around with a dramatic flourish.

"This is the home of Lyle LaFarge," she announced importantly. "Creator of the the toasty-oat goodness of Jolly Rogers, and the spicy crunch of Cinnamon Rogers."

"Who cares about him Toots," hooted Scratchy, "where's the vittles?" The other pirates jeered in agreement.

"Naturally," Fay continued, ignoring the interruption, "Mr. LaFarge is constantly working to improve the crunchy goodness of Jolly Rogers cereal, so naturally, he has plenty of boxes on hand to experiment with."

"We want FOOD!" yelled Larko, from the back of the jostling pirate mob.

"What I'm about to give you is better than food," said Fay, trying hard not to look at Barnaby lest he be encouraged to open his mouth. She did not need interference from Hootsman as she set the stage for her spiderweb.

"I think you've flapped yer' mouth for long enough Missy," growled Yellow Tooth. "Time to show what yer' good for. Whar' be the Jolly Rogers?"

"If you'll follow me inside quietly," said Fay. "Because if Mr. LaFarge is adding just the right amount of crunch, or just the right touch of cinnamon...you don't want to mess him up."

"This oughta' be good," said Barnaby with a smirk. "What's today's special flavor? Snail snot?"

Fay turned and glared at him, her finger pointed accusatorially. "IT just might be," she said, "if we throw off his concentration with comments like that Hootsman. But I want to feed my mates right!"

Fay entered the house in an exaggerated tiptoe, followed by Barnaby who mimicked her step, his face contorted by a goony grin. To Fay's great amazement the pirates followed without their usual rude clamor, until someone shrieked.

It was Tilly, who was standing in the

kitchen doorway with Lynette on her hip.

"I knew it was true!" said Tilly accusingly. "You did join the pirates!"

"Aw, we already knew that," said Skipper, switching on the television. "Look at this."

On the screen a reporter, standing in front of Fipple's Florist, poked her microphone at Judy Fipple's father Horace Fipple.

"What's your reaction to reports that the outlaws have recruited local schoolchildren into their ranks?" asked the reporter.

"Children joining criminal gangs?" answered Mr. Fipple. *"This behavior is completely inappropriate. My daughter would never do that. I'd question the child-rearing methods of those parents. Yes I would...oh...and we're running a special on petunias--two for one low price!"*

"See?" said Skipper. "Now you're in really big trouble. Mom and Dad already got called to school to talk about you using Mr. Squibbly's intercom without permission or something."

"Fay!" scolded Tilly. "How could you bring them here? They're so not hot!"

The twelve pirates turned toward Tilly as a group and said *"Rrrrrrrg!"*

"Uggy yuck!" said Lynette.

"FOOD!" yelled the pirates, who were shoving each other, and completely filled the LaFarge's living room.

"I was just getting to that," replied Fay. "Skipper, you know where Dad keeps the *special* boxes of Jolly Rogers?"

Skipper looked a little confused. "The special boxes?"

"The special ones," repeated Fay. "The ones Dad makes *extra delicious* with his flavor testing kit?"

"Oh yeah, the flavor testing kit we're not allowed to touch," said Skipper with a growing smile. "The extra delicious Jolly Rogers. They're in the basement."

"That's right," said Fay. "Right next to the

flavor testing kit. Would you check just to make sure they really are extra delicious?"

"You bet," said Skipper. He disappeared down the stairs.

Yellow Tooth focused a narrow gaze on Fay. "I hope," he said ominously, "you're plannin' to feed us missy. And soon."

"FOOD!" yelled the other pirates.

Several minutes later, Skipper's voice rang from below. "Yum! This cereal is EXTRA delicious!"

"Maties," said Fay, "Let's chow down."

22

"Wait!" called Fay as the pirate band made ready to stampede down the basement stairway. "We've got a few more boxes here in the kitchen!" She tossed an armful toward the mob, and soon the empty-handed pirates were growling at their shipmates who'd made a catch.

"Don't worry," said Fay. "There's plenty for everyone downstairs."

"Okay LaFarge," said Barnaby, with a little less of his usual pesky confidence. "What happens when they scarf it all and are still grumpy?"

"Maybe," she replied mysteriously, "this will be our last pit stop. Just wait and see."

"Arrrrrr," came Yellow Tooth's satisfied growl from the basement. "I likes me little prize!"

"I want a prize!" whined Scratchy, as Fay and Barnaby crept halfway down the basement stairs.

"I'm sorry to say," said Skipper, who was now backing slowly up the stairs, "that the special boxes are here for flavor improvement experiments and they don't have prizes."

"No prize?" said Larko, squinting at the kids on the stairs. "I don't get me own Flippin' Eights?"

"No Eights?" said Hanky. He scooped a large handful from his box, and tried, unsuccessfully, to get it all in his mouth at once. "Pleehhhh!" Hanky spat, spewing Jolly Rogers everywhere. "Plehhh! Plehhh! Me cereal tastes like deer food! Horse poo! Cow paddies!"

"Goose doodoo!" added Scratchy, who also had one of the test boxes.

Hanky glared around at his comrades. "I'll be having YOURS," he said, snatching an upstairs box of cereal from Lizard.

"Hey!" protested Lizard, but he hardly had time to react before Scratchy lunged at Buttercup and wrested the cereal box prize from his grasp.

"Them's my Flippin' Eights!" hollered Buttercup. "Give me back my Flippin' Eights!"

"If you like horsey-doo eat it yourself!"

shouted Jimbo, shoving a handful of bad experimental cereal into Hatch's mouth.

Fay led the quiet retreat up the basement steps.

"Nice job making those boxes extra tasty, Skip," she whispered to Skipper. "Now, while they're busy killing each other we lock the door..."

"Get the heck outa' here," added Barnaby.

"And call the cops," said Skipper.

"Tilly, grab Lynette and let's go!" said Fay. She opened the front door right into the knee-high boots of Mr. Arg.

"Let's step back inside Missy," said Mr. Arg fixing her with his most withering glare. "It seems I need to have a word with your Poppa about his light-fingered young'un."

23

Fay looked suspiciously at her fingers.

Mr. Arg was now completely blocking the only exit.

"Light fingers," he said with a frightening grin. "The sort what lift things that aren't theirs."

"What?" said Barnaby. "Like pirate coins?" He nodded his smirking face at Fay.

"Ooooh..." said Mr. Arg, "sounds familiar does it?"

"Pirate coin?" said Fay, backing up, and trying to sound as naive as she could, even though she'd had a feeling from the moment that coin tumbled out of the Cinnamon Rogers Box that it wasn't supposed to be in there.

"Hey guys?" said Skipper, shaking Fay's arm. "I think they're trying to get out of the basement!"

Fay glanced at the basement door. Someone was jiggling the doorknob from the other side. "Mr. Arg," she said, "any chance we could talk about this somewhere else? You really don't want to be here right now."

"But I do," said Ms. Parsnip pushing her way in the front door.

She squared off in front of Mr. Arg with her hands on her hips as he staggered back a step.

"I want to have this discussion right now! What were you thinking by subjecting schoolchildren to the dangerous conditions we experienced today?" she demanded. "I've more than half a mind to report you to the proper authorities, but I thought you might like a chance to explain!"

"Shifty woman!" exclaimed Mr. Arg. "You've

been follerin' me?"

"And it seems I'm not the only one," replied Ms. Parsnip.

"HEY!" bellowed Yellow Tooth from behind the basement door. "What you bloody tryin' ta do? Lock us in?"

"MISTER Arg!" came the shrill voice of Mrs. Pink as she imperiously pushed her way past Ms. Parsnip.

Mr. Green and Mr. Brown strode in behind her looking very grim.

Mrs. Pink waved her mobile phone in Mr. Arg's face. "I had my doubts when they put you in charge of Crunch & Barley. Oh, yes I did. But I held my tongue, and now look what's happened! I need only push ONE BUTTON to put me in touch with the fraud investigator! Do you or do you not have an explanation for the inventory deficiency?"

"OPEN the blasted DOOR!" screamed Yellow Tooth, his voice getting angrier.

Fay was on the verge of panic. Her spider

web was going horribly wrong. "Mr. Arg!" she said. "They're going to break down the..."

"DON'T try to change the subject Missy!" interrupted Mr. Arg.

"Mr Arg!" said the increasingly ruffled Miss Parsnip. "You are a public safety hazard!"

"Mr. Arg!" warned Mrs. Pink. "See my finger? It's about to push a button!"

"AAAARRRRRRG!" The basement door crashed onto the living room floor, its frame in splinters.

Yellow Tooth loomed in the doorway, his ugly frame leaving only tiny spaces where Jimbo and Scratchy peered through, scowling.

"So it's ARRRG as is trying to lock us up, is it now?" said Yellow Tooth in an oily voice, as he coolly drew his cutlass from its scabbard.

"I didn't lock you up you scurvy sack o'cat litter, but I'll shake the hand of him what did!" replied Mr. Arg.

"Her," said Barnaby, pointing at Fay. "Her

what did."

Yellow Tooth fixed his beady gaze on Fay. "Why you backstabbin', mutineering, little piranha," he growled. "Maybe you'd be tasty spit-roasted!"

Miss Parsnip shook her finger at the pirates who were pushing and shoving their way out of the basement stairwell.

"You don't work with children at all well," she said. "I hope you don't think you'll be invited back for Pirate Day next year! You really can't control your behavior, can you?"

There was jostling and grumbling from the rear of the pirate mob.

"Me Flippin' Eights cup is busted!" whined Hanky. "Larko stepped on me Flippin' Eights cup!"

"You can play with mine," offered Buttercup helpfully, "soon as ol'Yellow is done making mincemeat outa' Arg!"

"What say you booooyy?" said Yellow Tooth,

addressing Mr. Arg in what Fay took to be a most disrespectful manner. "Have it out wif' me right here! Right here in this pretty room." He pointed his cutlass menacingly, and took a few practice swings at the air.

"Yeller, you pit-faced blowfish," replied Mr. Arg, standing his ground with equal ferocity. "I don't need to fight to win back me crew's loyalty!"

An evil grin materialized on Yellow Tooth's face. "Yer' muvver was a cod's liver," he challenged.

"A what?" demanded Mr. Arg.

"Ya' heard me the first time," replied Yellow Tooth. "A cod's liver. And she wore smelly stockings!"

Fay barely saw Mr. Arg move, but in the space of a second he'd sprung from the doorway to squarely in front of Yellow Tooth. His sword cut the air with a whoosh, and crashed, in earsplitting ferocity, into Yellow Tooth's cutlass.

"Me mum..." said Mr. Arg. *(CRASH!)*

"Did the laundry..."*(CLANG!)*

"Every Tuesday..."*(WHAP!)*

"And her stockings..."*(BANG!)*

"Smelled *(WHOOSH!)* like *(CLANK!)* LAVENDER!" *(CRASH!)*

The kids, Miss Parsnip, and the Board of Directors backed away in horror, but the pirate mob was almost salivating. One moment it seemed that Arg had the upper hand. The next it seemed that Yellow Tooth would surely skewer him.

"HEY!" yelled Tilly who was trying to shrink but still couldn't hide her indignation. "You pug-uglies are dinging the walls! Mom hates dinged walls!"

"Ding waws!" yelled Lynette. "Pug uggy!"

Mr. Arg's sword sliced at what little hair there was on Yellow Tooth's head. "You," he charged, "are a yeller-bellied, pansy-faced, mutinous mud-sucker!"

"And YOU," cried Yellow Tooth with a

mighty swing which knocked Mr. Arg's sword right out of his hand, *"are a shish-kebab!"*

Fay stared as Mr. Arg's sword crashed to the ground in what seemed like horrifying slow motion. She could not tear her eyes away from what she fully expected to be guts spilling on the living room floor.

Yellow Tooth laughed, a horrible growly laugh, and he leveled his blade at Mr. Arg's throat. "I'm afraid there won't be no Davy Jones to welcome you back to the locker Arg. You want to be skewered fast or slow?"

"NEITHER ONE!" bellowed Mrs. Pink impatiently shoving the point of Yellow Tooth's cutlass away and stepping in front of Mr. Arg. "Mind your manners you blithering barbarian! You're not depriving me of the satisfaction! I've been waiting a long time for this collar!"

A growl rose in Yellow Tooth's throat as he glowered at Mrs. Pink, and Fay fully expected the cutlass to do its bloody work on both Pink and

Arg, but instead, he lowered his blade and the first crack of a grin glimmered on his lips. "You ain't no lady," said Yellow Tooth. The grin grew bigger. "No, you ain't no lady...yer' a scorpion!"

Mrs. Pink looked at Yellow Tooth with a smile that seemed both coy and deadly. "Yes," she replied. "A scorpion. About to make a sting."

"AS AM I!" roared Yellow Tooth, suddenly turning his attention, and cutlass toward Fay.

Fay had never seen such a horrible leer, and backed away, almost falling over Barnaby.

"Hurry it up!" hollered Hanky. "Whack'er head off! We wants ta' play wif' the Flippin' Eights in peace and quiet!"

All that Fay could see beyond Yellow Tooth's beefy frame was the plastic cup, from the cereal box toy, which Hanky was waving in the air as he whined.

"But Hanky!" she yelled, playing the one desperate card she had left. "You lost your squidger!" She dug into her pants pocket. The coin was still there.

"Me squidger?" whined Hanky. "I lost me squidger?"

"Don't worry!" called Fay, pulling out the pirate coin. "You can have mine!"

Fay wished, and hoped, and threw---like a girl. As the pirate coin sailed over Yellow Tooth's confused head, Fay grabbed Skipper by one arm, Barnaby by the other, and yanked them along to plow Tilly, Lynette, Miss Parsnip, and, quite by accident Mr. Arg, out the front door.

In the split second before the screen door slammed shut, she hoped beyond hope that the *"plink"* she heard was Mr. Arg's coin landing in Hanky's plastic cup, and the whooshing sound was a vortex that wouldn't take no for an answer.

24

Fay skipped the Cinnamon Rogers and ate eggs for breakfast. At school, she entered her classroom to find Barnaby Hootsman staring at her through the wrong end of a plastic spyglass.

"Fay LaFarge!" he hooted. "You're two inches tall!"

"Hootsman!" she replied. "You should've been a swabby!"

"Now now, boys and girls," interrupted Miss Parsnip, giving the unmistakable hand signal that meant "everyone sit down." "Yesterday's field trip was so fraught with mishap that I never had the chance to tell you about my great-great-great

Auntie Bonny Patty Parsnip!"

"Swell," whispered Fay to Franny. "I was so hoping she'd gotten pirates out of her system by now."

Miss Parsnip caught Fay in a teacherly glare.

"Fay LaFarge," said Miss Parsnip. "You and Barnaby were the only children who saw the re-enactors' exhibit. What can you tell us about Bonny Patty?"

"She ran a store," Fay replied. "With her father."

"A useless store," cut in Barnaby. "No Pepsi, no trading cards, no atomic fireballs..."

Donny Bing waved his hand above his head. "How many kinds of soup did they sell in the olden days?" he asked.

"It wasn't a soup store," replied Fay.

Judy Fipple's hand shot up next. "It wouldn't have been a flower shop either," she said. "Cut flowers can only be safely transported and preserved using modern refrigeration."

"If you ask me," said Barnaby, "It was a pickle store."

"It was a general store," said Fay. "Until the pirates burned it down."

"Yes," said Miss Parsnip with a nod. "According to Parsnip family legend it was when Bonny Patty lost her store in a pirate raid, that she commandeered an abandoned ship and became a buccaneer herself."

"That's crazy," said Fay. "Did she have a crew?"

"Ah yes," said Miss Parsnip with a strange and wistful sigh, "she acquired a crew...but at first there was only her paramour."

"Pair of what?" asked Barnaby.

"Paramour," said Miss Parsnip. "Boyfriend, lover, first mate...his name was Roger McCorley."

"McCorley?" said Fay with a choke. "More mass, go get garbage McCorley?"

"If he had a nickname like that," answered

Miss Parsnip sternly, "I was certainly unaware of it."

"How desperately romantic," enthused Judy Fipple. "I hope they had a beautiful wedding...with flowers."

Barnaby jumped out of his seat and danced a swooning jig, his hands preciously clasped. *"Romance, romance,"* he sang. *"Oh lovely romance!* Too bad it'll never happen to you Fay LaFarge."

"Too bad you're going to fall in the mud on your way home Hootsman," replied Fay.

"Now now," chided Miss Parsnip, "you two remind me of another part of Elbow Harbor pirate lore."

"The muddy part?" asked Barnaby.

"The wicked part," responded Miss Parsnip, giving the "settle down class" hand signal. "The part about Bonny Patty's rivals on the high seas. The bloodthirsty Captain Yellow Tooth and his mysterious first mate, The Pink Scorpion."

"The Pink Scorpion," cooed Judy Fipple with obvious admiration.

"Mind you," said Miss Parsnip. "She was as cutthroat as they come. With those two on the loose, Bonny Patty defended harbor towns as often as she hunted treasure."

"The Pink Scorpion," said Fay with a knowing glance at Barnaby, who smirked in acknowledgment.

"There now, boys and girls," sighed Miss Parsnip. "It's been a lovely legend to share, but we must get on with our schoolwork...and I musn't be late tonight. I have a dinner date, at Chez Crispette."

"Miss Parsnip!" exclaimed Fay. "Who are you going out with?"

"That's for me to know," replied Miss Parsnip coyly. "Fractions class!"

25

Things were really messy at the Crunch & Barley Breakfast Factory. In Lyle LaFarge's flavor lab a scrawny man stirred the contents of a beaker with sloppy enthusiasm.

"Um...Mr. Twicky," said LaFarge wiping orange batter from his labcoat, "there'll be more for us to taste if you can keep it in the beaker."

"Won't taste right if it ain't mixed right," replied Twicky. He wiped a claw-like finger across a blob of batter on his name badge which said, "Mr. Twicky--Flavor Lab," stuck it in his mouth, and licked his lips appreciatively. "Never thought about that afore."

"Thought about what?" asked LaFarge.

"Injun squash in Pappy's hardtack," replied Twicky. "Who thunk it up?"

"We're not quite sure who put squash in the cereal dough," answered LaFarge.

"Good thinkin'," continued Twicky, "but lousy batter--cain't make decent hardtack outa' gruel. Lucky thing ya' shanghaied me."

"LaFaaar-r-r-ge!"

That familiar voice from the hallway snapped LaFarge's attention away from Twicky and the batter-splattered lab.

"Mr. Arg," said LaFarge, nodding to his boss.

Mr. Arg looked like he knew a secret. "So," he said with a nudge and a wink, "how's me new Crunch & Barley spesh-ee-ality shaping up?"

"Oh," replied LaFarge, "Squashy-Tack. We think we'll have it ready for distribution in a week or two."

"And will them fancy grown-ups like it?"

LaFarge felt an unusual surge of confidence. "Squashy-tack fuses old-fashioned sustenance with a modern flavor twist--I, for one, anticipate strong sales."

"Strong sales," repeated Mr. Arg with a sly smile. "Oughta keep the Board of Dee-rectors outa my hair."

"Have you met the new Board yet sir?" asked LaFarge.

Mr. Arg blew through his lips like a horse and shook his head. "No tellin' what kinda porridge-suckers and tea-sippers the stockholders will have picked out," he said. "But I got me ace in the hole. That rule what says I gets to pick one of 'em out meself. Someone who thinks a little like me, maybe."

"That's terrific sir," said LaFarge, wondering if it was, in fact, at all terrific. "So who did you pick?"

"That's fer me ta' know LaFar-r-r-ge," replied his boss. "Cain't discuss it right now. Gots ta' git home and comb me whiskers...Going to a fancy-britches dinner at Chez Crispette."

Twicky stopped stirring and cackled. "The cap'n's dallying with ladies, eh? Who's the muffet?"

Arg growled through a tightlipped smile. "That," he said, "is fer me ta' know too."

****

At breakfast the next morning, Skipper got the spyglass, and Lynette got the Flippin' Eights. Tilly got a glimpse of the hot United Delivery guy who brought an urgent letter to the kitchen door.

But it was Fay LaFarge who got the urgent letter. An opportunity. An invitation. A position as the "kid consultant" on the Crunch & Barley Cereal Factory Board of Directors.

Fay shoveled a large spoonful of Cinnamon Rogers into her mouth, and considered. Maybe it was time to stop looking out only for herself.

She'd just saved her family from being shish-kebabed after all. Maybe now she could look out for everyone who ever ate Jolly Rogers cereal.

"Yep," she said. "I'll take it."

Made in the USA
Middletown, DE
30 May 2020